Let's Go, Hoosiers!

Aimee Aryal

Illustrated by Anuj Shrestha

MASCOT BOOKS

It was a beautiful day at
Indiana University.

Two little Hoosier fans were on their way
to Assembly Hall to watch a basketball
game. Let's follow them to the game!

The little Hoosiers walked past the
Student Building and stopped at
Rose Well House.

A professor passing by said,
"Let's go, Hoosiers!"

The little Hoosiers passed by
Indiana Memorial Union.

A group of students standing outside yelled, "Let's go, Hoosiers!"

The little Hoosiers stopped
at Beck Chapel.

A couple walking by said,
"Let's go, Hoosiers!"

The little Hoosiers walked by
the Main Library.

A librarian who works inside waved
and said, "Let's go, Hoosiers!"

It was almost time for the basketball game. As the little Hoosiers walked to the game, they passed by some alumni.

The alumni remembered going to
basketball games when they went to IU.
They said, "Let's go, Hoosiers!"

Finally, the little Hoosiers arrived
at Assembly Hall.

They watched the team run onto
the basketball court. The crowd cheered,
"Let's go, Hoosiers!"

The little Hoosiers watched the game
from the stands and cheered
for the team.

The Hoosiers scored a basket!
The players shouted,
"Slam dunk, Hoosiers!"

At halftime the Big Red Basketball Band
performed for the crowd.

The little Hoosiers sang
"Indiana, Our Indiana."

The Indiana Hoosiers won the game!

The little Hoosiers gave the coach
a high-five. The coach said,
"Great game, Hoosiers!"

After the basketball game, the little
Hoosiers were tired. It had been a
long day at Indiana University.

They walked to their homes and
climbed into their beds.

"Goodnight,
little Hoosier fans."

For Anna and Maya,
and all little Hoosier fans. ~ AA

For Rajani and Ivan, who helped me find a home in Queens,
and carried me through this new chapter in my life.
Thank you, mero pagal sathi haru. ~ AS

Special thanks to:

Robin Cooper and the I.U. Licensing Department

www.mascotbooks.com

©2012 Mascot Books, Inc. All Rights Reserved. No part of this publication may
be reproduced, stored in a retrieval system or transmitted in any form by any
means electronic, mechanical, or photocopying, recording or otherwise without
the permission of Mascot Books, Inc.

For more information, please contact:
Mascot Books
560 Herndon Parkway #120
Herndon, VA 20170
info@mascotbooks.com

ISBN-13: 978-1-937406-78-3
ISBN-10: 1-937406-78-4
CPSIA Code: PRT0612B

INDIANA UNIVERSITY, IU, HOOSIERS are trademarks or registered trademarks
of Indiana University and are used under license.

Printed in the United States

Have a book idea?

Contact us at:

Mascot Books
P.O. Box 220157
Chantilly, VA 20153-0157

info@mascotbooks.com | www.mascotbooks.com

TM

Look and Find

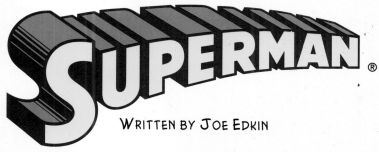

®

WRITTEN BY JOE EDKIN

ILLUSTRATED BY JAIME DIAZ STUDIOS

COVER CHARACTER ILLUSTRATION BY GRAHAM NOLAN

SCENES 3 AND 6 COLORED BY ADRIENNE ROY

PUBLISHED BY
LOUIS WEBER, C.E.O.
PUBLICATIONS INTERNATIONAL, LTD.
7373 NORTH CICERO AVENUE
LINCOLNWOOD, ILLINOIS 60646

COPYRIGHT © 1996 DC COMICS. ALL RIGHTS RESERVED.

SUPERMAN CREATED BY JERRY SIEGEL AND JOE SHUSTER

SUPERMAN AND ALL RELATED CHARACTERS AND THE LIKENESSES THEREOF,
SLOGANS, ELEMENTS, AND INDICIA ARE TRADEMARKS OF DC COMICS.
THIS BOOK MAY NOT BE REPRODUCED OR QUOTED IN WHOLE
OR IN PART BY ANY MEANS WHATSOEVER WITHOUT WRITTEN
PERMISSION FROM THE COPYRIGHT OWNERS.

MANUFACTURED IN CHINA.

8 7 6 5 4 3 2 1

ISBN 0-7853-3943-4

LOOK AND FIND IS A REGISTERED TRADEMARK
OF PUBLICATIONS INTERNATIONAL, LTD.

PUBLICATIONS INTERNATIONAL, LTD.

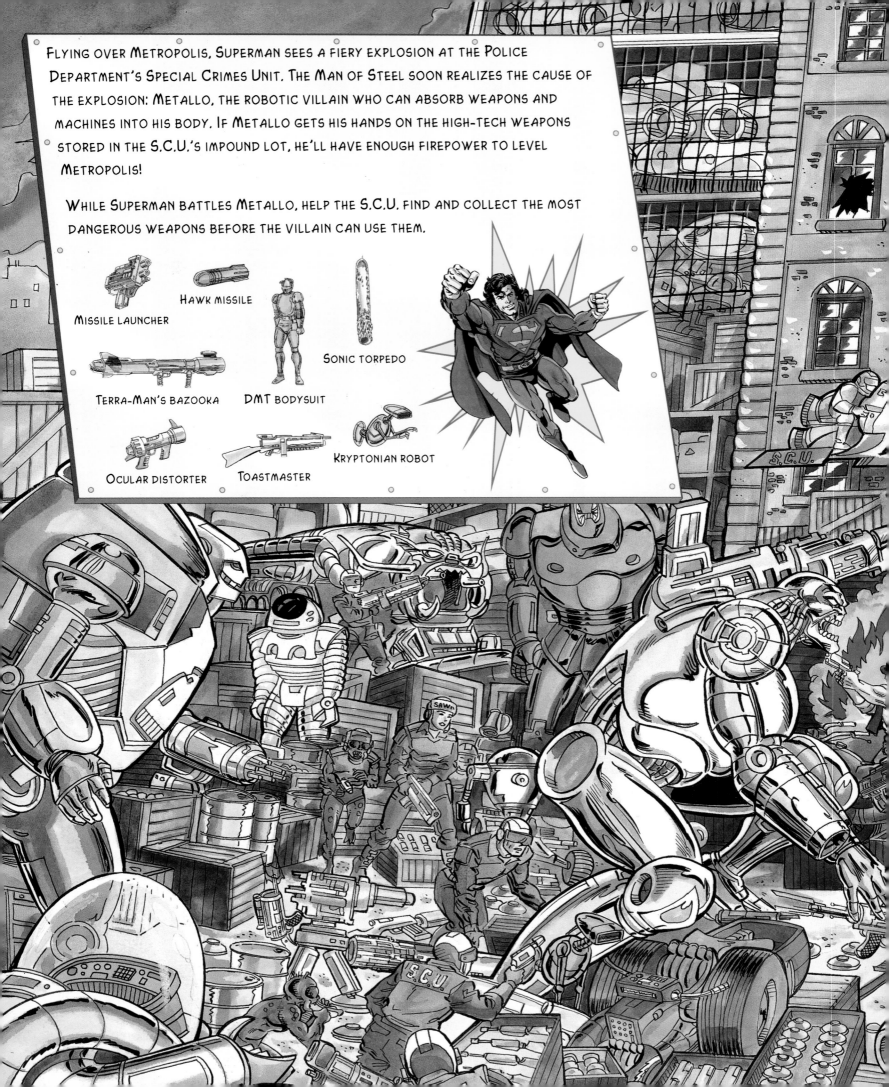

FLYING OVER METROPOLIS, SUPERMAN SEES A FIERY EXPLOSION AT THE POLICE DEPARTMENT'S SPECIAL CRIMES UNIT. THE MAN OF STEEL SOON REALIZES THE CAUSE OF THE EXPLOSION: METALLO, THE ROBOTIC VILLAIN WHO CAN ABSORB WEAPONS AND MACHINES INTO HIS BODY. IF METALLO GETS HIS HANDS ON THE HIGH-TECH WEAPONS STORED IN THE S.C.U.'S IMPOUND LOT, HE'LL HAVE ENOUGH FIREPOWER TO LEVEL METROPOLIS!

WHILE SUPERMAN BATTLES METALLO, HELP THE S.C.U. FIND AND COLLECT THE MOST DANGEROUS WEAPONS BEFORE THE VILLAIN CAN USE THEM.

MISSILE LAUNCHER

HAWK MISSILE

TERRA-MAN'S BAZOOKA

DMT BODYSUIT

SONIC TORPEDO

OCULAR DISTORTER

TOASTMASTER

KRYPTONIAN ROBOT

AFTER DEFEATING METALLO, SUPERMAN DISCOVERS THAT THE IMPOUND LOT HAS BEEN INFESTED WITH DEADLY MAN-SIZED BUGS KNOWN AS HELLGRAMMITE SPAWN. SUPERMAN CHASES THE CREATURES INTO SUICIDE SLUM, ONE OF METROPOLIS'S MOST DANGEROUS NEIGHBORHOODS. AS SUPERMAN HOPED, THEY LEAD HIM TO THE HELLGRAMMITE'S HIDEOUT. THE EVIL HELLGRAMMITE HAS WRAPPED UP EIGHT PEOPLE IN COCOONS IN ORDER TO TRANSFORM THEM INTO ITS WRETCHED SPAWN. THE HELLGRAMMITE HAS ALSO WRAPPED UP SEVERAL DECOYS IN COCOONS. SUPERMAN MUST USE HIS X-RAY VISION TO LOCATE THE HELLGRAMMITE'S VICTIMS.

HELP SUPERMAN FIND THE EIGHT REAL CAPTIVES BEFORE THEY ARE TRANSFORMED.

GABBY

DUBBILEX

TOMMY

FLIP

BIG WORDS

SCRAPPER

GUARDIAN

BOBBY

JUST AS SUPERMAN CAPTURES THE HELLGRAMMITE AND FREES ITS VICTIMS FROM THE COCOONS, HIS SUPERHEARING DETECTS AN ALARM GOING OFF AT STRYKER'S ISLAND PRISON. THIS IS SHAPING UP TO BE A BUSY DAY!

SUPERMAN DISCOVERS ONE OF HIS MOST POWERFUL ENEMIES, CONDUIT, DESTROYING THE PRISON—JUST TO GET THE MAN OF STEEL'S ATTENTION. CONDUIT KNOWS SUPERMAN IS ALSO DAILY PLANET REPORTER CLARK KENT, AND THE VILLAIN HAS AN OLD GRUDGE TO SETTLE. TO GET HIS REVENGE, CONDUIT HAS PLANTED NINE CLUES THAT WILL REVEAL SUPERMAN'S SECRET IDENTITY TO THE WORLD!

HELP SUPERMAN FIND THE FOLLOWING ITEMS, SO HE CAN THEN STOP THE BREAKOUT AND DEFEAT CONDUIT.

CLASS PRIZE

CLARK KENT'S GLASSES

LOIS LANE

FOOTBALL TROPHY

YEARBOOK

SUPERMAN DUMMY

PICTURES OF JONATHAN AND MARTHA KENT

VARSITY JACKET

SUPERMAN HAS WON THE BATTLE AGAINST CONDUIT, BUT THERE IS NO TIME TO REST. S.T.A.R. LABS, THE HIGH-TECH RESEARCH CENTER, IS UNDER ATTACK. THE DEADLY PARASITE HAS BROKEN OUT OF HIS CONTAINMENT CELL. WITH JUST A TOUCH, HE CAN KILL AN ORDINARY PERSON OR DRAIN SUPERMAN'S POWERS!

THE MAN OF STEEL CRASHES INTO THE LAB TO CONFRONT THE PARASITE. THINKING FAST, SUPERMAN LOOKS FOR METAL ITEMS THAT HE CAN MELT DOWN AND USE TO BIND THE VILLAIN. HE HAS TO BE VERY CAREFUL; JUST ONE TOUCH AND HE COULD BE FINISHED.

HELP SUPERMAN FIND THE FOLLOWING METAL ITEMS SO HE CAN CAPTURE THE PARASITE.

FILE CABINET

WATER HEATER

SAFE

STEEL BARREL

METAL SHELF

STEEL BEAM

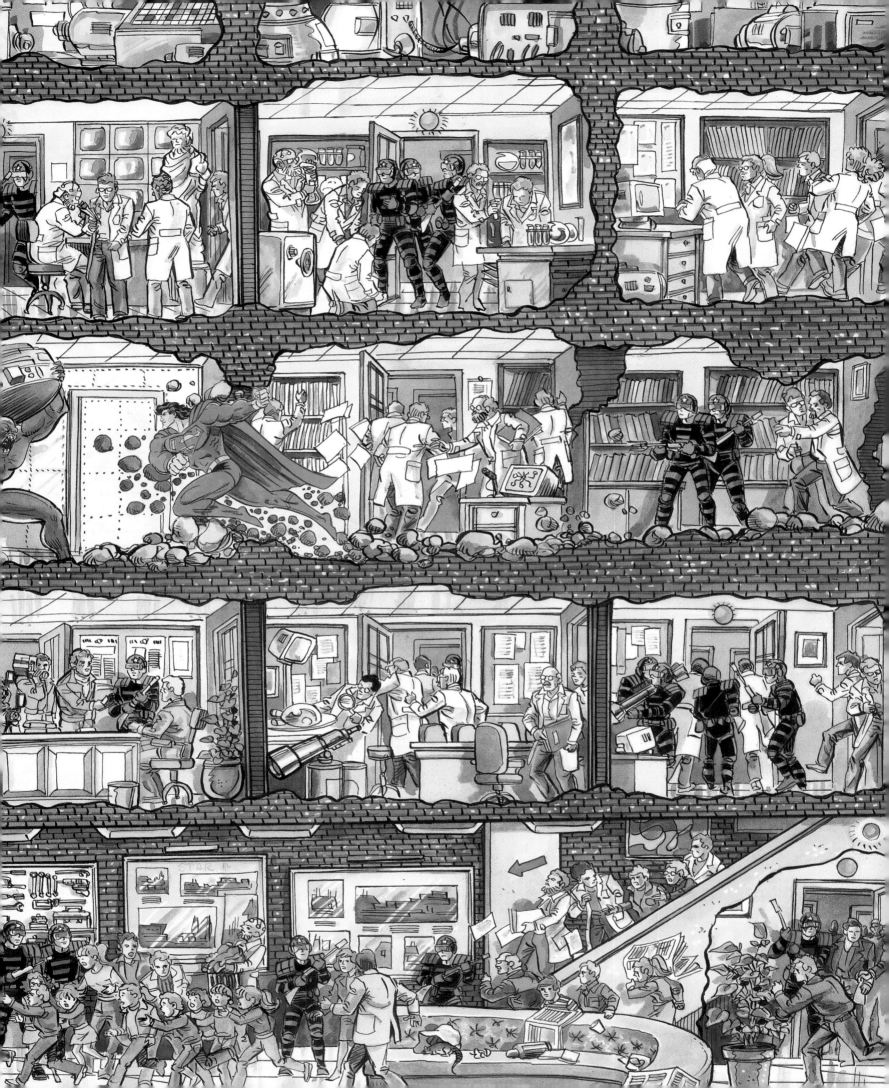

After returning the Parasite to his cell, a tired Superman flies into space to get closer to Earth's sun, which gives him his strength. But above the atmosphere two of his deadliest enemies—Mongul and the Cyborg—block his way.

Mongul, the intergalactic tyrant, has fired 14 missiles from his ship, seven of which are heading straight for Metropolis. Meanwhile, the vicious Cyborg is attacking a nearby space station, leaving the astronauts stranded in the vacuum of space.

Help Superman find the astronauts while he uses his heat vision to destroy the seven missiles rocketing toward Earth.

Sergeant Pittarese

Missile

Commander Siegel

Lieutenant Duffy

Sergeant McAvennie

Captain Shuster

THE CYBORG HAS FLED INTO THE DEPTHS OF SPACE, BUT MONGUL CONTINUES TO ATTACK, BLASTING SUPERMAN WITH HIS LASERS. SUPERMAN FIRES BACK WITH HIS HEAT VISION AND DAMAGES MONGUL'S SHIP, WHICH SPIRALS TOWARD EARTH AND CRASHES INTO METROPOLIS'S HOB'S BAY.

SUPERMAN FOLLOWS MONGUL UNDERWATER AND DISCOVERS THAT A HUGE HOLE IN THE SHIP HAS SCATTERED MONGUL'S COLLECTION OF DEADLY WEAPONS IN THE POLLUTED WATERS.

HELP SUPERMAN FIND THE WEAPONS BEFORE MONGUL DOES, SO THAT HE CAN PREVENT THE EVIL ALIEN FROM USING ANY OF THEM AGAINST METROPOLIS.

EXPLOSIVE SHURIKEN

OKAARAN CONCUSSION GRENADE

MATTER BLASTER

KHUND BAZOOKA

TAMARIAN FIRE CANNON

ZAMARONIAN MISSILE LAUNCHER

NUCLEAR MINE

DURLAN SONIC DISRUPTER

HOPING TO GET SOME REST, SUPERMAN FLIES TOWARD THE *DAILY PLANET* BUILDING. THERE, HE SEES PANIC IN THE STREETS. IT'S DOOMSDAY — THE MONSTER THAT ONCE NEARLY PUT SUPERMAN OUT OF ACTION FOREVER! SOMEHOW, HE HAS MADE HIS WAY BACK TO METROPOLIS.

SUPERGIRL, SUPERBOY, STEEL, AND THE ERADICATOR ARE ALREADY ON THE SCENE, BUT EVEN THESE POWERFUL SUPER HEROES AREN'T ENOUGH TO STOP THE MONSTER'S RAMPAGE. MANY INNOCENT BYSTANDERS ARE IN GREAT DANGER.

HELP THE OTHER HEROES FIND AND RESCUE THESE PEOPLE WHILE SUPERMAN DEFEATS DOOMSDAY'S ATTACK.

JOE

RON TROUPE

PERRY WHITE

TRACY

JIMMY OLSEN

OFFICER O'HARA

LOIS LANE

FIFTH

CO

SUPERMAN IS EXHAUSTED AND CONFUSED. WHY ARE SO MANY VILLAINS ATTACKING IN ONE DAY? SUDDENLY, HE HEARS A HIGH-PITCHED LAUGH OVER AT THE HAPPYLAND AMUSEMENT PARK. IT'S MR. MXYZPTLK, THE MAGICAL PRANKSTER FROM THE FIFTH DIMENSION WHO CAN DO ALMOST ANYTHING WITH HIS MAGIC. WHAT HE LOVES TO DO MOST IS USE HIS POWERS AGAINST SUPERMAN. IT WOULD BE JUST LIKE HIM TO CONJURE UP ALL THOSE VILLAINS.

MR. MXYZPTLK OFFERS SUPERMAN A BARGAIN: HE HAS PLANTED SEVERAL LETHAL "JOKES" AROUND THE PARK. IF THE MAN OF STEEL FINDS THEM ALL BEFORE ANYONE GETS HURT, MR. MXYZPTLK WILL DISAPPEAR AND UNDO ANY DAMAGE HE HAS CAUSED. HELP SUPERMAN FIND ALL THE "JOKES," SO HE CAN SEND THE IMP BACK TO THE FIFTH DIMENSION.

A DANGEROUS BOUQUET

KILLER COTTON CANDY

A WILD STUFFED ANIMAL

A VERY HUNGRY LION

AN EXPLODING HOT DOG

A BERSERK BALLOON

A DEADLY CAN OF PEANUTS

AN UNFUNNY FUN HOUSE MIRROR

Petting Zoo

OF LOVE

Having beaten Mr. Mxyzptlk at his game, Superman expects the day to return to normal. Instead, things become even stranger! Brainiac, the master of mental manipulation, has invaded Superman's mind, creating a disturbing "mindscape."

"It was I you were fighting all along," taunts Brainiac. "The dangers you faced today were all illusions of my creation."

Superman is surrounded by images of his friends in danger. To overcome this villain, Superman must use his last reserves of strength and courage to rescue his friends and regain control of his mind. Help the Man of Steel find his friends so that he can shatter the illusions and defeat Brainiac once and for all!

Steel

Superboy

ShadowDragon

Thorn

Supergirl

Gangbuster

Guardian

Agent Liberty

Superman has defeated Brainiac and put an end to the villain's mayhem. But if you go back, there is still more for you to do.

While Superman fought Metallo, there were creepy, bug-like Hellgrammite Spawn hiding in the S.C.U. impound lot. Can you go back and find the spawn:

- ☐ Lurking behind boxes
- ☐ Hiding under a car
- ☐ Eating a hot dog
- ☐ Playing a game
- ☐ Listening to music
- ☐ Impersonating an officer

Back in Suicide Slum, find the following fire hazards before they cause trouble.

- ☐ Gas can
- ☐ Can of turpentine
- ☐ Box of matches
- ☐ Burning cigar
- ☐ An unattended stove
- ☐ exposed wires

During the confusion at Stryker's Island Prison, several inmates tried to escape. Find the prisoners trying to escape by:

- ☐ Digging a hole
- ☐ Hiding under a blue blanket
- ☐ Filing the bars
- ☐ Climbing a wire
- ☐ Dressing like a woman

To cause even more trouble, Brainiac put several scientists at S.T.A.R. Labs under his control. They are all wearing special headbands. Can you find the following scientists:

- ☐ Looking through a microscope
- ☐ Writing an equation
- ☐ Sweeping
- ☐ Tasting a potion
- ☐ Welding steel parts
- ☐ Taking out the garbage